# JEREMY STRONG

# Nellie Choc-Ice

## Penguin Explorer

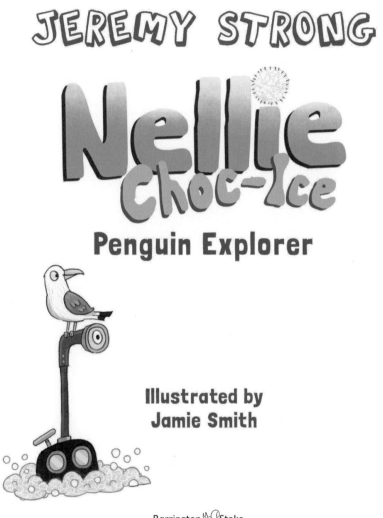

### Illustrated by
### Jamie Smith

Barrington Stoke

First published in 2017 in Great Britain by
Barrington Stoke Ltd
18 Walker Street, Edinburgh, EH3 7LP

www.barringtonstoke.co.uk

Text © 2017 Jeremy Strong
Illustrations © 2017 Jamie Smith

The moral right of Jeremy Strong and Jamie Smith to be
identified as the author and illustrator of this work has been
asserted in accordance with the Copyright, Designs and
Patents Act, 1988

A CIP catalogue record for this book is available
from the British Library upon request

ISBN: 978-1-78112-721-6

Printed in China by Leo

This book is in a super readable format for young readers
beginning their independent reading journey.

*This is for penguins everywhere.*
*I hope it will help pass the time during*
*those long Antarctic winters.*

# Contents

# Chapter 1

# The penguin explorer

This is Nellie Choc-Ice. As you can see, she is a penguin. There are several different kinds of penguin, just as there are different kinds of people. Nellie Choc-Ice is a Macaroni Penguin. If you don't believe me you can look up 'Macaroni Penguin' online and you will see lots of lovely pictures.

You might be wondering why she is called Nellie Choc-Ice. Grand-Pa Penguin is to blame for that. When she was a new little penguin just hatched from her egg, Grand-Ma Penguin asked her mum and dad what her name was.

"Nellie," Small-Ma said, and Small-Pa nodded.

"She's much more than a plain Nellie," Grand-Ma complained. "Look at that lovely white chest and glossy black wings. She looks just like an ice-cream covered with dark chocolate."

"Nellie Choc-Ice!" Grand-Pa chuckled.

"Nellie Choc-Ice!" Small-Pa beamed.
Small-Ma thought it was a very good
name too.

The fluffy bundle at their feet gazed up at her family. "Nellie Choc-Ice!" she squeaked and then she fell over. That was because she had only just been born and was small and weak. I expect you used to fall over a lot when you were small.

Nellie liked to be an explorer from the moment she was born. She mostly explored the rocky ground around her. This was because she still fell over a lot.

As Nellie grew older she explored the sea too. She was better at that because you can't fall over underwater. Don't try it yourself – you're not a penguin. You CAN try it if you ARE a penguin.

Soon Nellie was on her feet all the time.  She loved visiting her family.  It was a large family.  Nellie had hundreds of brothers and sisters, aunts and uncles, nephews and nieces, great-aunts, great-uncles, little-aunts and little-uncles – not to mention one very small uncle who wore a hat and played the guitar.

Nellie loved exploring so much that she soon climbed to the top of several very big icebergs that no other penguins had ever climbed before. In fact, some of her family asked her why she bothered.

"Because I can!" Nellie laughed. "Because they're there!"

Then the other penguins would look at her and say, "Oh Nellie!  You ARE a penguin!"

And Nellie thought that was even funnier because of course she WAS a penguin, so why did they bother to tell her?

Anyhow, it wasn't long before Nellie Choc-Ice became the most famous penguin explorer, ever. You can't check that online, but I tell you it's true. You can believe me because I'm a writer.

You might now be wondering how Nellie became so famous. You ARE wondering, aren't you? If you don't want to know then you may as well go and read something else, like "The Very Boring Adventures of a Penguin that Didn't Do Anything".

What a waste of time that book would be, and not very interesting at all. It would be much better for you to stick with this book. That is because the story of World Famous Penguin Explorer Nellie Choc-Ice is very interesting.

In fact, in the next chapter the story of Nellie Choc-Ice gets VERY EXCITING, so please carry on.  Thank you.

## Chapter 2

# The story of Nellie Choc-Ice gets very exciting

Nellie wasn't afraid of anything except killer whales. Killer whales eat penguins, so it was a good thing that Nellie was scared of them. There are a lot of killer whales in the oceans around Antarctica.

You do know that penguins live around the Antarctic, don't you?  It's a pretty wild place.  It is full of snow, ice and wind and it's VERY cold.  Sometimes it is SO cold it makes your toes turn black and fall off, unless of course you are a penguin.

Anyhow, one day Nellie Choc-Ice was standing on the ice, in the wind, looking out to sea.  She was puzzled.  Something thin and black was coming towards her, little by little.

Nellie decided that it was a man walking across the water.

But it wasn't. It was the periscope from a submarine. Nellie had good eyesight but she had never seen a submarine before, so it's not surprising she made a mistake.

Then the top part of the submarine appeared – the bit that's called the conning tower.

"It's a man a long way away," Nellie told herself. "He's walking on the water and now he's carrying a suitcase."

Then the water started to boil up around the conning tower. It sloshed about and all of a sudden the WHOLE SUBMARINE popped up onto the surface of the sea.

"No no no no no NO!" Nellie Choc-Ice cried. "It's a KILLER WHALE and it's coming to EAT ME!"

Poor Nellie was so scared she ran away as fast as she could. She jumped onto the nearest iceberg and climbed to the very top.

But as Nellie stood at the top, the iceberg wobbled. A big crack opened up down one side. The iceberg split in two and the biggest part began to drift away into the open sea. That was the part of the iceberg that had Nellie Choc-Ice clinging to the top. Oh dear. What was she to do?

Meanwhile, inside the submarine, a man with an enormous beard was staring into his periscope. The man's name was Rear Admiral Captain Beardy-Beard. He wasn't called a Rear Admiral because he sat at the back of the submarine. In fact, I don't know why he was called a Rear Admiral at all, but he was.

I think we shall just call him 'Captain' now and forget about the Rear Admiral bit. I'm sure he won't mind.

But I DO know why his name was Beardy-Beard. When he was a little baby his granny sat him on her lap and said, "One day this boy will grow up and have a big, beardy beard."

And he did, so his granny was right.

Anyhow, Captain Beardy-Beard was peering through his periscope to see what was going on.

"I can see a penguin going for a ride on an iceberg," he told his crew. "That is so sweet."

And all the crew lined up to have a look into the periscope.  They laughed and smiled a lot.  That evening they wrote emails to their families.  One said –

*Dear Mum, Saw a penguin riding on an iceberg today.  It looked fun.  Love from Charlie.*

But it wasn't fun for Nellie at all.
She was all alone. She was miles out at
sea and she didn't know where she was
going. As it grew dark, Nellie wondered
if she would ever see her family again.

## Chapter 3

## Will Nellie ever see her family again?

The iceberg drifted along with a miserable Nellie sitting on top, all by herself.  Where were all her lovely relatives?  They were a long way away.

The Antarctic was now far behind and the distance between the land and the iceberg was growing day by day.

The weather grew warmer and the iceberg began to melt. Nellie's icy island was shrinking. Oh dear. How alarming.

One day a large gull landed on top of the iceberg. He didn't even say "hello" to the little penguin before he started to chip chunks off the edge of the iceberg. (You have probably noticed that gulls have very bad manners. I blame their parents.)

"Could you stop that, please?" Nellie asked, because she was a polite and well-brought-up penguin. "The sun is melting my iceberg and if it melts away to nothing I shall have no home."

"Then fly away and find another one," the gull said, and he chipped off another chunk of ice.

"I can't fly," Nellie pointed out. (Did you know penguins can't fly? Of course you did.)

But the gull didn't know.  He was only interested in stealing sandwiches and ice cream cones from small children, or pecking at icebergs in order to annoy little penguins.  He stopped and looked at Nellie.  "Don't be ridiculous," he said. "You're a bird.  Birds fly."

"I know," Nellie said.  "But I'm a penguin and penguins can't fly."

"That is the most stupid thing I have ever heard," the gull declared.  "What is the point in a bird that can't fly?"

Nellie stiffened her shoulders and gave the gull a severe look.  "I swim.  I'm a very good swimmer."

The gull laughed so much he fell off
the top of the iceberg. "You SWIM!" he
said. "That is ridiculous!"

"It's not ridiculous at all," Nellie snapped. "I can swim very well. In fact, swimming is just like flying except you do it underwater. Can YOU swim underwater?"

"I don't need to because I can fly," the gull sniggered. He was feeling very clever.

"Huh!" Nellie snorted. "Fancy not being able to swim underwater. Now that IS ridiculous."

"I'm not ridiculous, you're ridiculous!" the gull shouted.

Nellie Choc-Ice stamped her little feet. "Can't swim! Ha ha! Ridiculous!"

The gull's eyes flashed. "You pesky penguin! I'll get you!"

The gull dived down at Nellie, stabbing at her spitefully with his nasty beak. But Nellie simply plunged into the sea where she was safe.

The gull flew round and round, wondering where she had gone. At last he grew bored and flew off.

Nellie flipped back onto her little icy island. "Huh!" she grunted, as she gave her wings a quick shake. "Gulls! They're such bossy-beaks!"

The sun shone. The day grew hotter and Nellie's world was melting away to nothing!

# Chapter 4

# Will Nellie's world melt away to nothing?

Nellie didn't realise that the iceberg had drifted so far north it had crossed the Equator. She was more than half way round the world!

Her icy home was now so small she could barely stand on it. It wobbled too, as if it might tip right over at any moment. Nellie was worried.

But then a strange thing happened. The weather grew colder day by day. One morning Nellie woke up covered in frost. Then she spotted another iceberg, a big one, and then another and another. At last she saw land – and it was full of SNOW AND ICE!

"I'm home!" Nellie shouted. She hopped onto land and looked around for her big penguin family. She searched everywhere but she couldn't see a single relative, not even Small-Ma or Small-Pa.

Nellie wandered about sadly until she found a large white rock to sit on. It was like a warm, furry cushion. Nellie pushed her chilly feet into the soft surface.

"Oh!" Nellie cried as the rock got to its feet, lifted her into the air and she slid off.  Nellie found herself staring into the dark, black-as-night eyes of a VERY large polar bear.

Nellie looked at the bear's big mouth and flashing teeth.  She saw the bear's huge paws and long claws and took two steps back.

"Who and what are you?" the bear demanded.

"I'm a penguin," Nellie said bravely. "My name is Nellie Choc-Ice. What's yours?"

"Hungry," the bear growled.

Nellie managed a smile. "That's an unusual name," she said. She was scared but she tried hard not to show it.

"I haven't eaten for three days," the bear went on.  He leaned towards her and sniffed.  "You smell of meat," he said.  "I like meat."

"Meat is bad for you," Nellie declared.  "Vegetables are much better. If you want to be healthy you should eat vegetables.  Green stuff."

The polar bear looked around at the endless snow and ice. "Ffff!" he grunted. "I can't see any green stuff. No vegetables in the Arctic." He bent over Nellie and sniffed harder.

"I'm sure some will come along soon," Nellie said brightly. She inched towards a small hole a seal had made in the ice. She stood at the edge and peered into it.

"There's green stuff in here," Nellie pointed out.

"Really?" the bear growled. He sighed, stumped across to the hole and looked. "I can't see any green."

"It's down there, at the bottom. You need to get closer," Nellie told him.

The bear peered more deeply into the hole.  Nellie crept behind him. Just as the bear muttered that he still couldn't see any green Nellie leaned all her weight against the bear's back.  She pushed and pushed with her feet.

"OH!" the bear cried as he toppled into the hole.

He plunged head-first into the water and right away got stuck as his large tummy became wedged in the hole. All Nellie could see was his bottom and his back legs waggling madly in the air. A frantic gurgling bubbled up from below the ice.

"NELLIE CHOC-ICE!"

But the little penguin had already disappeared. Unfortunately she had run away so fast she had no idea where she was. She was completely lost in Nowhere Land.

# Chapter 5

# Lost in Nowhere Land

"I'm lost and I'm hungry," Nellie told herself. "I don't have a map, so I'll try and find some fish to eat first."

She hunted around for a seal hole that didn't have a polar bear in it.

Soon she spotted a small lump of snow that kept moving about.  That was because it had four legs and – bad news for Nellie – it was an Arctic fox.

"Well, hello there," said the fox. "What plump yummy-thing have we here?"

"I'm Nellie Choc-Ice," Nellie said stoutly. "I'm a penguin. I'm looking for my family – Small-Ma and Small-Pa, my brothers, sisters, cousins, aunts, uncles –"

"Stop!" the fox cried. "Too much information. Anyhow, you won't find them here."

"I won't?" Nellie's heart sank.

The fox shook his head. "You're a penguin. Penguins live at the South Pole. This is the North Pole. You're a long way from home. Twelve thousand, four hundred and thirty miles to be precise."

Nellie almost fainted. "I've come that far?" she whispered.

The fox picked at his teeth with one sharp claw.  His tummy gave a low rumble.

"I can help you find your way back." The fox smiled.

"Really?"

"Oh, sure," the fox said. "Head for the ocean and then go south. Simple. I've heard that penguins swim. You can't fly, can you? I mean you can't take off and escape?" The fox grinned. "Sorry, I don't mean escape. I mean, what is there to escape from here? Nothing dangerous, it's not like I want to EAT you or anything crazy like that."

The fox gave Nellie a very innocent look.

The look was so innocent that Nellie felt alarm bells jingle all over her. She didn't know much about other animals but she did know what meat-eating teeth looked like and the fox had a pretty snappy set of them.

Nellie looked around. There wasn't a seal hole in sight and it's hard to run away from a fox when you've got short legs and massive flippers for feet. Oh dear. What was she to do?

"If you could show me the way to the ocean that would be very helpful," Nellie said.

The fox cheered up. "Of course. Follow me, please."

Have you noticed how polite that fox
is?  You see, even when someone has
good manners it doesn't mean that they
are a good person.  Nellie had better
watch out.

So, Nellie shuffled along beside the
fox and he looked at her and licked
his lips.  Nellie felt rather like she
was about to be someone's dinner and
wondered how she could escape.

# Chapter 6

# How can Nellie Choc-Ice escape?

Soon Nellie and the fox came to a seal hole. The fox had a good drink. When he had finished he turned to Nellie.

"You should drink too," he told her. "Don't worry. I shall keep watch right beside you."

Nellie knew that as soon as she bent down to drink, the Arctic fox would jump on her and grab her. Her brain was working hard on a plan.

Nellie went to the seal hole. Just as she bent down to drink she saw the fox move towards her. Quick as a flash she dived into the hole. Down she swam to the bottom. But when she looked back up she could see the fox's head peering into the hole, just waiting for her to come back.

Nellie began to swim back up to the seal hole. Faster and faster she went until she was zooming up through the water like a tiny, penguin-shaped rocket.

Then WHOOSH! BAM! Nellie exploded out of the hole. She knocked the Arctic fox flying. He went somersaulting backwards – 23 somersaults! It was probably a world record, for a fox. You could look it up in the Big Book of World Records.

Nellie landed back on the snow. The Arctic fox was out cold. Nellie hurried on to the sea and suddenly THERE IT WAS.

A vast grey ocean stretched in front of her. Twelve thousand, four hundred and thirty miles to home. Could she really swim that far?

NO.

Nellie sat down. She thought how she would never see her family again and great big tears plopped onto the snow at her feet.

As Nellie gazed out to sea she saw
something thin and dark on the water.
At first she thought it might be a man,
far away.

Then something big and black came
out of the water and Nellie decided it
must be a man with a suitcase. But
then the water boiled and foamed and a
submarine popped up on the surface of
the sea.

Poor Nellie.

She had escaped a polar bear and an Arctic fox, but now that killer whale was after her again. She fainted on the spot.

Of course, you know it wasn't a man with a suitcase or a killer whale. It was the very same submarine that Nellie had seen before.

Rear Admiral Captain Beardy-Beard looked out of his periscope.

"My goodness me," he said to his crew. "There's that penguin again, the one we saw at the South Pole. How on earth did she get here? We had better take her home to Antarctica."

And that is exactly what they did.

Some of the crew sent emails to their families.  One said –

*Dear Mum*

*We have rescued a penguin called Nellie Choc-Ice and we are taking her back home.  She is cute, except when she poops on my lap.*

*Lots of love, Charlie.*

And there we are.  What an adventure for a small penguin.  Nellie Choc-Ice became famous overnight. Newspapers had headlines like this –

PENGUIN FOUND AT NORTH POLE!

Nellie was even on TV.

But Nellie's adventures were not over.  You see, on the way back to Antarctica, the submarine had to stop at all sorts of places and Nellie got into quite a lot of trouble.  So did Captain Beardy-Beard.  But that's another story.

Our books are tested
for children and young people by
children and young people.

Thanks to everyone who consulted on
a manuscript for their time and effort in
helping us to make our books better
for our readers.